KU-200-372

This igloo book belongs to:

....

igloobooks

Published in 2019
by Igloo Books Ltd
Cottage Farm
Sywell
NN6 0BJ
www.igloobooks.com

Copyright © 2016 Igloo Books Ltd
Igloo Books is an imprint of Bonnier Books UK

All rights reserved. No part of this publication may be
reproduced or transmitted in any form or by any means,
electronic, or mechanical, including photocopying, recording,
or by any information storage and retrieval system,
without permission in writing from the publisher.

0719 002.01
2 4 6 8 10 9 7 5 3
ISBN 978-1-78905-659-4

Written by Melanie Joyce
Illustrated by Sanja Rescek

Cover designed by Lee Italiano
Interiors designed by Justine Ablett
Edited by Hannah Cather

Printed and manufactured in China

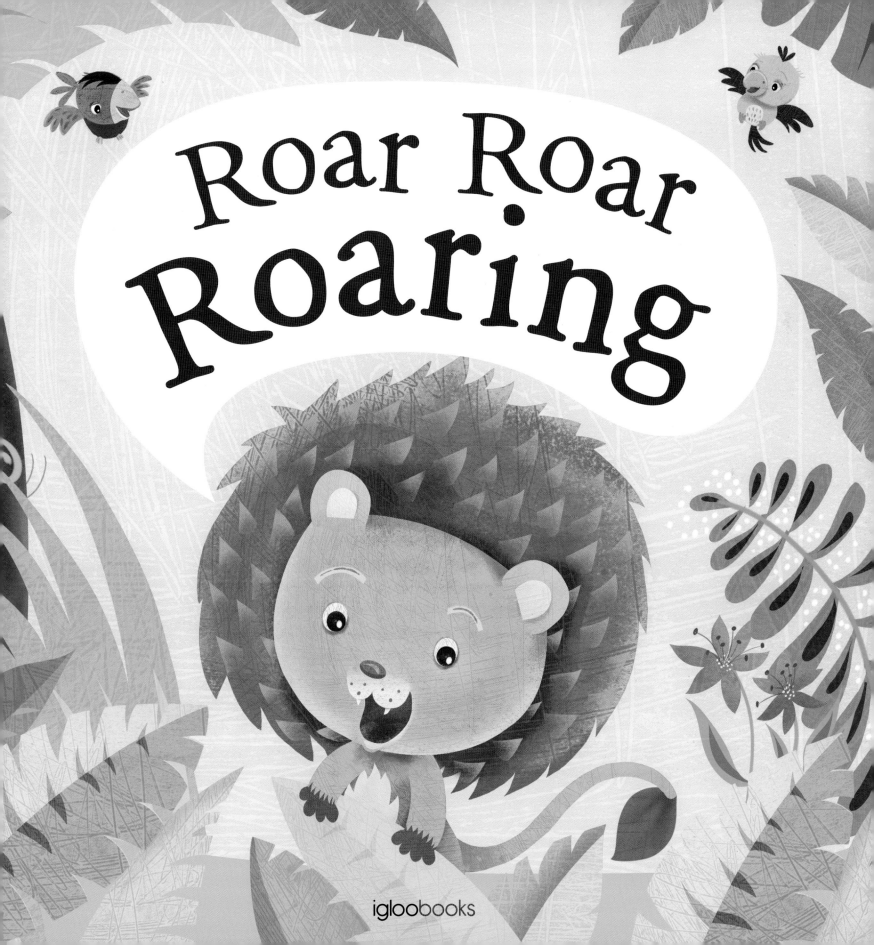

Roar Roar Roaring

igloobooks

Lion is in the jungle, roar-roar-roaring, waking up the animals, snore-snore-snoring.

ROAR!

Roar goes Lion and shakes his shaggy mane.
Squawk go the parrots. Squawk, they go again.

It's a **roar-snore-Squawk** noisy jungle day.

The monkeys all start **swing-swing-Swinging**, **oo-oo-ooing** as the birds are **singing**.

ROAR!

Tweet-tweet-tweet go the birds all around.
Oo-oo go the monkeys, swinging to the ground.

It's a swing-oo-oo-tweet noisy jungle day.

The zebra chews the grass and it's **yum-yum-yummy.**
He **chomp-chew-Chomps** and fills up his tummy.

It's a **clomp-Stomp-Chomp** noisy jungle day.

The hippo in the mud is gloop-gloop-glooping...

... sinking slowly, bloop-bloop-blooping.

The **swishy** little fish all **wiggle** their fins.
They all **splash** out, then **sploosh** back in.

ROAR!

It's a **gloop-bloop-splash** noisy jungle day.

The gorillas all giggle, **jump-jump-jumping,**
beating on their chests, **thump-thump-thumping.**

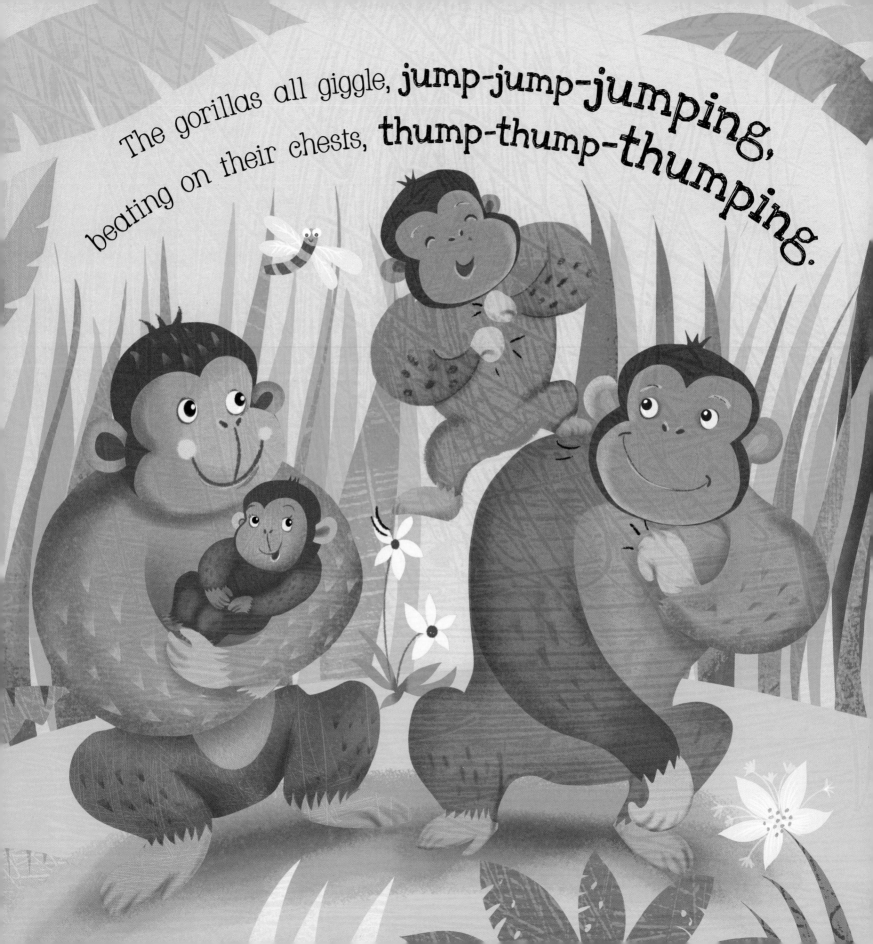

Hiss-hiss-hiss goes a snake, sneaking past, slithering and sliding in the long grass.

ROAR!

It's a jump-thump-hiss noisy jungle day.

A toothy crocodile is **creep-creep-Creeping** past the leopard, who is **sleep-sleep-Sleeping.**

ROAR!

SNAP goes the crocodile.
SNAP, SNAP,
SNAP.

He wakes up the leopard from his cosy nap.

It's a **creep-sleep-Snap** noisy jungle day.

The little elephants are **play-play-playing.**
Their curly trunks are **sway-sway-swaying.**

It's fun to **splash** in the waterfall.

Whoosh go the elephants, trunks and all.

ROAR!

It's a **play-sway-splash** noisy jungle day.

The cheetahs run by, **chase-chase-chasing**,
all around the jungle, **race-race-racing**.

The giraffe is happy to
munch-munch-munch,
nibbling at the high leaves,
crunch-crunch-crunch.

It's a chase-race-crunch
noisy jungle day.

Soon the sun is glow-glow-glowing,
above the river that's flow-flow-flowing.

Everyone is tired after all that play.
They've had such a lovely jungle day.

It's a **glow-glow-flow** noisy jungle day.

Lion and the parrot stop **roaring** and **squawking**.
There's no more **swinging** or **stomping** or **clomping**.
No more **glooping**, **blooping** or **jumping**.

No more creeping, sleeping, playing, thumping, swaying, chasing, racing, munching, crunching.

Sleep-sleep-**Snore** is the only jungle sound.